Mr. Scruff

SIMON JAMES

CANDLEWICK PRESS

First U.S. edition 2019

Library of Congress Catalog Card Number pending
ISBN 978-1-5362-0935-8

19 20 21 22 23 24 CCP 10 9 8 7 6 5 4 3 2 1

Printed in Shenzhen, Guangdong, China

This book was typeset in Minion.
The illustrations were done in ink and watercolor.

Candlewick Press
99 Dover Street
Somerville, Massachusetts 02144

visit us at www.candlewick.com

This is Polly.

She belongs to Molly.

This is Eric.

He belongs to Derek.

This is Minnie.

She belongs to Vinnie.

But who's this?

It's Mr. Scruff. . . .

For Mr. Scruff there's no one.

This is Mick.

He belongs to Rick.

And this is Lawrence.

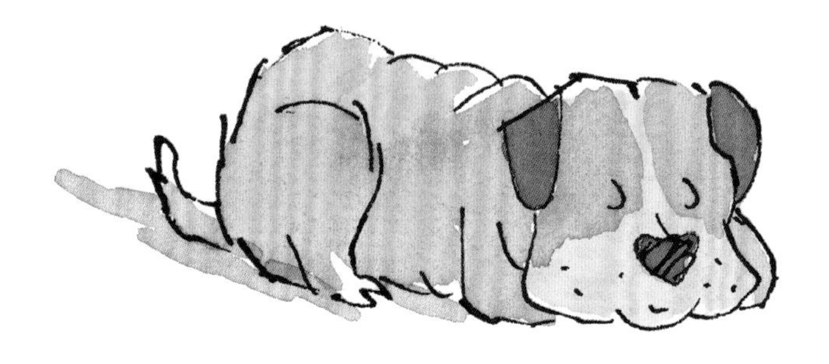

He belongs to Florence.

But things are looking rough
for poor old Mr. Scruff.

Wait a minute! Who's this?

It’s Jim!

They seem to like each other.

"But Jim," says Dad,
"are you sure?
He's so BIG,
and you're so small!
I can't see it working.
No, not at all!"

"He's so OLD," says Mom,
"and you're so young.
Surely a puppy would
be more fun?"

“No,” says Jim.
“He needs a home.
A place to call his very own.
That’s what he needs.
And that’s enough
for me—
and Mr. Scruff.”

So, while
Polly has Molly,
Eric has Derek,
Minnie has Vinnie,
Mick has Rick,
and Lawrence has Florence,
now . . .
Mr. Scruff belongs to Jim!

And though it doesn't rhyme,
it's all worked out just fine.

But wait a minute. Who's this?

It’s Mr. Gruff.
He’s come to choose a dog.

Here's a little pup.
They seem to like each other.

"I'm so BIG,
and you're so small.
But that doesn't matter.
No, not at all!"

Mr. Gruff is happy.
It's the perfect
dog for him.

Can you guess the puppy's name?
Well, of course—

it's Tim!